MW00887903

For Nick and Ruth, and Liz and David –
achoos to dedicate this book to you, with loads of love – **S.P.**

For Mum (who taught me to cover my nose when I sneeze) X – **N.R.**

BLOOMSBURY CHILDREN'S BOOKS
Bloomsbury Publishing Plc
50 Bedford Square, London, WC1B 3DP, UK
29 Earlsfort Terrace, Dublin 2, Ireland

BLOOMSBURY, BLOOMSBURY CHILDREN'S BOOKS and the Diana logo
are trademarks of Bloomsbury Publishing Plc

First published in Great Britain 2022 by Bloomsbury Publishing Plc

Text copyright © Simon Philip 2022
Illustrations copyright © Nathan Reed 2022

Simon Philip and Nathan Reed have asserted their rights under the Copyright,
Designs and Patents Act, 1988, to be identified as the Author and Illustrator of this work

All rights reserved. No part of this publication may be reproduced or transmitted in any form
or by any means, electronic or mechanical, including photocopying, recording, or any
information storage or retrieval system, without prior permission in writing from the publishers

A catalogue record for this book is available from the British Library

ISBN 978 1 5266 2372 0 (HB)
ISBN 978 1 5266 2373 7 (PB)
ISBN 978 1 5266 2362 1 (eBook)

13 5 7 9 10 8 6 4 2

Printed and bound in China by Leo Paper Products, Heshan, Guangdong

To find out more about our authors and books visit www.bloomsbury.com and sign up for our newsletters

AcHoO!

SiMON PHiLiP

Illustrated by NATHAN REED

THIS WAY...

BLOOMSBURY
CHILDREN'S BOOKS
LONDON OXFORD NEW YORK NEW DELHI SYDNEY

You probably know it's good manners to always say

thank you

and

please,

to cover your mouth if you're going to cough, and cover your nose when you sneeze.

But Sid, who could feel **his** nose twitching,

forgot and let loose an . . .

ACHOO!

And out of his nostrils flew something absurd . . .

...an **elephant**

in a canoe!

The elephant found a spare paddle,
and room on the boat for Sid, too.
But while Sid was paddling, his nose twitched again,
and out came another...

ACHOO!

It
caused
the
canoe
to
plunge
over
the
waterfall
in
the
ravine!

And out of Sid's uncovered nostrils there shot . . .

...a totally
tropical scene!

A ship that was swarming with

pirates –

their chief had a hook for a hand!
A coconut tree that leaned over the sea,
and **turtles** that basked on the sand.

While helping the pirates hunt treasure,
Sid found them a welcoming crew.

They finally got to where X marked the spot —
but then came another ...

ACHOO!

The pirates all cowered in terror,
alarmed at the size of Sid's sneeze.

You'll never suppose
what swung out of his nose . . .

...an **acrobat**

on a trapeze!

And Sid was soon in the performance –
together, they flipped and they flew;

they tumbled and twirled
and they wheeled and they whirled...

But then came another...

AcHoOO!

The clown and the dogs were distracted,

the juggler dropped all of his clubs,

and somehow, bizarrely,

Sid's nostrils shot out . . .

...a **panda**

with all of her cubs!

Bewilderment turned into chaos,

yet during the hullaballoo,

Sid's impulse to sneeze
seemed to finally ease...

But then came **another** . . .

AcHoO!

And that was the start of a **frenzy**

of sneeze after sneeze after **sneeze**,

as rapidly out of his nostrils there surged . . .

And then came

a giant,

a beanstalk,

a pair of untrustworthy **queens,**

some **princesses**

...fighting with peas!

a **COW** and a few magic beans.

STOP!

a **wolf** and a **mouse**

and a gingerbread house,

As Sid **tried** to work out what happened
(he hadn't the faintest of clues),
his sneezing fit eased so the things that he'd sneezed
made use of the gap in **achooos**.

Now everyone gathered together
and told Sid,

"Enough is enough!

Don't add to our woes!
Can't you **cover** your nose?!

You've **GOT** to stop sneezing this stuff!"

Sid listened and said he was sorry,
ashamed that he'd caused them such grief.
He **covered** his nose when a sneeze next arose,
to everyone's utter relief.

But just as they thought it was over,

the **elephant**
on the canoe

developed an itch

and he felt his trunk twitch . . .

And out came another . . .